Walter Crane

Queen Summer; or, the Tourney of the Lily & the Rose

Walter Crane

Queen Summer; or, the Tourney of the Lily & the Rose

ISBN/EAN: 9783337189143

Printed in Europe, USA, Canada, Australia, Japan

Cover: Foto ©Andreas Hilbeck / pixelio.de

More available books at **www.hansebooks.com**

Queen Summer
or the Tourney
of the Lily & the Rose
penned & portrayed
by Walter Crane

mdcccxci

Cassell & Co: Ld: London: Paris: & Melbourne

When Summer on the earth was queen
  She held her court in gardens green
Fair hung with tapestry of leaves,
Where threads of gold the sun enweaves
With chequered patterns on the floor
Of velvet lawns the scythe smoothes o'er:
Their waving fans the soft winds spread
Each way to cool Queen Summer's head:
The woodland dove made music soft,
And Eros touched his lute full oft.

3

Round Time's dial thronged the Hours,
Masking in the Masque of Flowers

Like knights and ladies fair be-dight
In silk attire, both red and white.

And as the winds about them played,
And shook the flowers or disarrayed,

A whispered word among them goes
Of how the Lily flouts the Rose,

Suitors for Summer's favour dear,
To win the crown of all the year —
And how each champion brave would fight
Queen Summer to decide the right.

Then shrill the wind-winged heralds blew;
The lists were set in Summer's view.

With blazoned shields, & pennons
Of fluttering flag & fleur· spruce
·de·luce :

And spread with 'broidered hangings
Till all was ready for the fray.   Say,

Between their banners white and red,
Of Rose and Lily overhead,
Queen Summer took her judgment seat,
Whom all the crowd of flowers did greet.

The silver arum-trumpets sound
With tongues of gold, & to the ground
The shining champions each did ride,
Their party-colours flaunting wide.

Came first the glowing Rose in view,
With crimson pennon fluttering new;
With glittering spines all armed he came,
With lance and shield—a rose aflame;
With tossing crest and mantling free,
On fiery steed,—a sight to see!

Nor long the Lily knight delayed;
In silver armour white arrayed,
He flashed like light upon the scene,
A lamp amid the garden green.
Milk-white his horse, & housings fair
With silver lilies shining there.

The summer winds the onset blew:
With level lance each champion flew,

And clashed together, mid a snow
Of petals on the grass below.

Pressed eager then the gazing rows:
Some cried "the Lily", some, "the Rose"
But while the Fate of battle hung,
Again the silver trumpets sung:

And, sudden charging from each side,
Of Roses and of Lilies ride
A host to still maintain the strife
For roses   or for   lilies' life

Rose favoured knights of maidens true,
Their pennons blushing with each hue
Of Rose-craft, since from wild thorn frail
Their order grew - through dark & pale
Of maiden-bloom to damask deep,
Or Gloire-de-Dijon that doth keep
Enfolded fire within his breast,
Still golden hearted like the rest.

Like a cloud of morn they bore,
Or rosy wave on grassy shore,
That, breaking, dashed the silver spray
They met - the Lily-lances play;
In crested legends on that came
Against them - snow & burning flame
Mixing with the crimson flood
Of roses & their fragrant blood,

Whereof the grass undue was rife,
As surged & rolled the Floral strife,
With chequered fortune o'er the green,
Until at last up— rose the Queen:

And caused the zephyr horns to blow
A truce, the victor's crown to show.
But like a garland on the ground
Of roses & of lilies found,
So linked & locked in strife they lay
Each silver stem & clinging spray,

The doughty champions could not rise
Before the Queen to claim her prize.
So to the field of battle down
She stepped, with rose & lily crown
Of silver & of gold fair wrought;
And thus Queen Summer spake her thought:

And to each warrior thus did say:
Read in the fortune of your fray
Fit emblem sweet of unity,
Nor Rose nor Lily plant on high,
But side by side in equal right,
And pleasant cheer the Red & White:

That men & maids be glad to see,
Alway in pleasant company,

Life & Love close linked together,
And strong to bear times wintry wea-
:ther

Love not consumed in passion's heart
But golden flamed & stedfast, sweet:

Time's snows shall quench not, though they hide:
Each spring renews the rosy tide:

Each lover in his lady's face
Sees roses blent with lilies' grace:

The poet & the painter praise
This heraldry of summer days;

And every garden sweet that blows
Doth set the Lily by the Rose.

Peace, then in all my borders be,
Beneath the silvern olive tree. "

Each rose, each lily's head bent low,
And each one sought his fallen foe:

And careful hands the wounded bore,
With balm and honey to restore:

35

And trimmed the grass & decked
And made all fit for dancers, each seat,
feet;

Beneath the summer full-orbed moon,
Ruddy & gold that rose full soon,
Like rose & lily fused in fire,
Ere the sunset's torch expire.

Then forth each knightly lily led
A blushing rosy dame so red;

Nor lily hands or hearts denied
The rose-hued warriors erst defied.

Light-footed through the dance's maze,
Quick they moved like wingèd fays;
As measured music soft did swell,
And echoed deep from bosky dell,
Till from the leafy forest side,
The sweet-tongued nightingale replied,
Dissolved in streams of silver sound,
Merged in the moonlight, lost & found;
Like the dancers, till in shade,
Of Summer's verdant night they fade.

BY THE SAME AUTHOR.

THIRD EDITION, price 5s.

FLORA'S FEAST:

A Masque of Flowers.

PENNED and PICTURED by
WALTER CRANE.

*With FORTY PAGES OF PICTURES, handsomely
reproduced in Colours.*

" The pictures are all charming. . . . This is the prettiest book
we have seen this Christmas."—*Pall Mall Gazette.*

" There is a long and splendid spectacle in the forty illustrations."—
Athenæum.

" This is a charming bit of fancy, of which we feel quite unable to
give any adequate description in words. The Snowdrops are accoutred
like warriors, with the bell-like flowers ingeniously adapted for helmets;
the Crocus is holding up his yellow cup flower; the Daffodils are
cleverly fashioned with huntsman's horns; Violet and Primrose are two
charmingly-attired sisters; and the rustic 'Maid Marsh Marigold,' with
a lamb at her side, is gay in gold and green. And so the poet-artist
goes through the year, with Roses of the garden and of the hedgerow;
Lilies, 'pale and proud,' or 'burning like an orange flame,' till at the
end of the long procession we come to the Christmas Rose. Mr. Crane's
skill with the pencil, graceful fancy, and tender and harmonious
colouring, have never found a more adequate expression than in this
charming volume."—*Spectator.*

CASSELL & COMPANY, LIMITED, *Ludgate Hill, London.*

A Classified Catalogue
OF
CASSELL & COMPANY'S PUBLICATIONS.

1d.
Cassell's Pocket Gardener.
Cassell's Penny Illustrated Stories. A Series of New and Original Stories. Illustrated. *(See also 2s. 6d. and 4s. 6d.)*
Historical Cartoons, Descriptive Account of.
Cassell's New Poetry Readers. Illustrated. 12 Books Each. *(See also 2s. 6d.)*
Cassell's Poetry for Recitation. (Suitable for Schools.)
The Scandinavian Plan. A Sermon on Intemperance, by the Ven. J. M. Wilson, M.A.

2d.
Scholars' Companion to Things New and Old.
Cassell's New Standard Drawing Copies. 6 Books Each. *(See also 3d. and 6d.)*
Cassell's Modern School Copy Books. 12 Books. Each.
Cassell's Graduated Copy Books. 12 Books. Each.
The Polytechnic Building Construction Plates. A Series of 40 Drawings. 15s. each.

3d.
Cassell's Brush Work Series. Series I. with FLOWERS. Series II.—PICTURES PAINTING WORDS. Series III.—ENTERTAINING PICTURES. 36 per set, each contains 19 Sheets. Each Sheet includes a Set of 3 Water Colours.
Cassell's "Belle Sauvage" Readers. An entirely New Series. Fully Illustrated. Strongly bound in cloth. Books 3 to 6, 1s. 6d. each.
Official Illustrated Railway Guides, Abridged and Popular Editions. Paper covers. Each. *(See also 1s. and 1s. 6d.)*
Great Western Railway.
Midland Railway.
Great Northern Railway.
London, Brighton and South Coast Railway.
Great Eastern Railway.
London and South Western Railway.
London and North Western Railway.
South Eastern and Chatham Railways.
CASSELL'S NATIONAL LIBRARY. Paper covers, 3d. each; cloth, 6d. *(A Full List of the 215 Volumes free on application.)*
Cassell's Readable Readers. Illustrated and strongly bound. Two Infant Readers at 2d. and 3d., and Six Books for the Standards, is very stiff cloth boards, at 3d. to 9d. *(List on application.)*
Cassell's Standard Drawing Copies. 6 Books. Each. *(See also 2d. and 6d.)*
Cobden Club Pamphlet. *(List on application.)*
"Building World" Coloured Plates. Each. *(Also in Sets of 6, 5s.)*
"Work" Coloured Plates. Each. *(Also in Sets of 6, 5s. Post free, 1s. 9d.)*

4d.
Cassell's "Eyes and No Eyes" Series. By Arabella Buckley. With numerous Illustrations and Coloured Plates. Books I. and II. *(See also 6d.)*
Lathe Construction. By Paul N. Hasluck. 12 Parts. Each, or 6s. per set.
Notes and Illustrations of the Essentials of House Sanitation. By Edward F. Willoughby, M.D., D.P.H.
The Wild Flower Collecting Book. (Complete in 6 Parts.)
The Wild Flowers Painting Book. (Complete in 6 Parts.)
Cassell's Standard Drawing Copies. 6 Books. Each. *(See also 2d. and 3d.)*
The Modern School Readers. Four Infant Readers at 3d. to 5d., and Six Books for the Standards at 7d. to 1s. 6d. *(Full List on application.)*
The Modern Reading Sheets. In Three Series, each containing Twelve Sheets in each. *(See also 6s.)*
Readers for Infant Schools, Coloured. 3 Books. Each. Containing 48 pages in Colours. Each.

6d.
EDUCATIONAL.
Cassell's "Eyes and No Eyes" Series. By Arabella Buckley. With numerous Illustrations and Coloured Plates. Books III., IV., V. and VI.
The Coming of the Kilogram. By H. O. Arnold-Forster, M.A.
A Practical Method of Teaching Geography. By J. H. Overton, F.C.S. Book I.—England and Wales, in Two Separate Parts. Vol. II.—Europe. Each. (Tracing Book, containing 40 maps, 4d.)
Shakespeare's Plays for School Use. Cloth. Each. Henry V. Hamlet. Julius Cæsar. Coriolanus. Richard II. King John. Merchant of Venice. Henry VIII.
Euclid, Cassell's First Four Books of. Paper, 6d.; cloth, 9d.
How to Draw Elementary Forms, Models, &c.
Spelling, Morell's Complete Manual of. *Cheap Edition.*
PEOPLE'S EDITION OF POPULAR NOVELS.
Black Arrow
The Master of Ballantrae } People's Edition. } By R. L. Stevenson.
Treasure Island } *(See also 3s. 6d. and 5s.)*
Kidnapped }
Catriona.
The Wrecker. By R. L. Stevenson and Lloyd Osbourne.
The Man in Black. By Stanley Weyman. *(See also 3s. 6d.)*
Dead Man's Rock. By A. T. Quiller-Couch. *People's Edition.*
The Splendid Spur. } (See also 3s. 6d.)
King Solomon's Mines. By H. Rider Haggard. *People's Edition.* Illustrated. *(See also 3s. 6d.)*
Father Stafford. By Anthony Hope.
The Man Wolves. } *(See also 3s. 6d.)*
The Iron Pirate. } By Max Pemberton.
Impregnable City. }
At Britain's Call. By S. Walker.
Adam Hepburn's Vow. By Annie S. Swan. *(See also 2s. 6d.)*
Out of the Jaws of Death. By Frank Barrett.
The Hispaniola Plate. By J. Bloundelle-Burton.
MISCELLANEOUS.
The National Gallery Catalogue. With upwards of 200 Illustrations.
The Catalogue of the National Gallery of British Art. *(The Tate Gallery.)* Profusely Illustrated. Net.
Cassell's Guide to Paris. Illustrated. *(Also 1s. 6d.)*
Cassell's Guide to London. Illustrated. *(Also 1s. 6d.)*
Cassell's Pictorial Guide to the Clyde. With Coloured Plates and Map. *(Also cloth, 1s.)*
Shall We Know One Another in Heaven? By the Rev. J. C. Ryle, M.A.
Cobden Club Pamphlets. *(List on application.)*
Lotta's Diaries. *(Also 1s.)*
Queen Victoria: Her Life in Portraits. Net. *(Also 1s. 6d.)*

6d.
To a Conning Tower; or, How I Took H.M.S. "Majestic" into Action. By H. O. Arnold-Forster, M.A. With Original Illustrations by W. H. Overend. *Cheap Edition. Cloth.*

7d.
Cassell's "High School" Readers. Illustrated and cloth.

8d.
Cassell's Modern Geographical Readers. From 1s.

9d.
ILLUSTRATED BOOKS FOR THE LITTLE ONES.
Bright Talks and Funny Pictures.
Merry Little Tales.
Little Tales for Little People.
Two Told for Sunday.
Sunday Stories for Small People.
Stories and Pictures for Bible Pictures for Boys and Girls.
Bright Stories.
The Cuckoo in the Robin's Nest.
The Twenty's Cradle.
Sunlight and Shade.
Rub-a-dub Tales.
Fine Feathers and Fluffy Fur.
Scrambles and Scrapes.
Tittle Tattle Tales.
Up and Down the Garden.
All Sorts of Adventures.
Our Holoiday House.
Creatures Tame.
Creatures Wild.
Those Golden Sands.
Cassell's New Geographical Readers. With Numerous Illustrations in each Book. From 9d. to 1s. 9d. each.

Things New and Old; or, Stories from English History. By H. O. Arnold-Forster, M.A. Illustrated. Cloth. Seven Books, from 9d. to 1s. 8d.

1/-
THE WORLD'S WORKERS.
John Cassell.
Richard Cobden.
Charles Haddon Spurgeon.
General Gordon.
David Livingstone.
The Earl of Shaftesbury.
Dr. Guthrie, Father Mathew, Elihu Burritt, Joseph Livesey.
George Müller and Andrew Reed.
Dr. Titus Salt and George Moore.
George and Robert Stephenson.
Charles Dickens.
Handel.
Turner the Artist.
Sarah Robinson, Agnes Weston, & Mrs. Meredith.
Mary Carpenter and Mrs. Somerville.
* The above works can also be had Twee in One Vol., cloth, 2s.
SMILING STORY BOOKS. All Illustrated, cloth 96d.
In the Days of King George.
Rhoda's Reward.
Fritz's Life Battle.
A Pair of Primroses.
Ella's Golden Year.
The Heiress of Wyvern Court.
Little Queen Mab.
Their Road to Fortune.
Won by Gentleness.
EDUCATIONAL.
"Work" Handbooks. A Series of Illustrated Practical Manuals prepared under the direction of Paul N. Hasluck, Editor of "Work." Each.
Decorative Designs of All Ages and for All Purposes.
House Decoration.
Bookbinding and Mounting.
How to Write Signs, Tickets, and Posters.
Wood Finishing.
Dynamos and Electric Motors, How to Make and Run Them.
Cycle Building and Repairing.
Mounting and Framing Pictures.
Latin Primer The First. By Prof. Postgate, M.A.
Howard's Art of Reckoning. *(Also 2s. and 3s.)*
Flowers, Studies in. In Thirteen Packets, each containing Six Sheets. Each Packet.
Euclid, Cassell's. First Six Books, with the 11th and 12th of Euclid.
German Reading, First Lessons in. By A. Jagst.
Polytechnic Technical Scales. Set of 20 in cloth case.
Smiths' Work.
Glass Working.
Building Model Boats.
Electric Bells, How to Make and Fit Them.
Bamboo Work.
Taxidermy.
Tailoring.
Photographic Cameras and Accessories.
Optical Lanterns.
Leatherio Work.
Repair Work.
Bookbinding.
CASSELL'S STANDARD LIBRARY.
Adam Bede. By George Eliot.
Wayward Ho! By Charles Kingsley.
The Last Curiosity Shop. By Charles Dickens.
Ivanhoe. By Sir Walter Scott.
The Last Days of Pompeii. By Lord Lytton.
Pride and Prejudice. By Jane Austen.
The Last of the Mohicans. By Fenimore Cooper.
American Humour. Selected.
Jane Eyre. By Charlotte Brontë.
Handy Andy. By Samuel Lover.
Uncle Tom's Cabin. By Harriet Beecher Stowe.
The Prince of the House of David. By the Rev. J. H. Ingraham.
* Complete List on Application.
MISCELLANEOUS.
Pictorial Practical Rose Growing. By Walter P. Wright. With 60 of 300 Illustrations. *(Also 2s. 6d.)*
Practical Greenhouse Management. By W. P. Wright. Illustrated. *(Also cloth, 2s. 6d.)*
Pictorial Practical Fruit Growing. By W. P. Wright. Copiously Illustrated. *(Also 2s. 6d.)*
The Army Business, and its London Office. By a Colonel in Business.
Queen Victoria: Her Life in Portraits. Net. *(See also 6d.)*
War Office, The. The Army and the Empire. By H. O. Arnold-Forster, M.A.
Dramatic Works of Lord Lytton.

1/- cont'd.

The Wallace Collection at Hertford House. By N. H. Spielmann. Illustrated.
Spending and Saving. By Alfred Pinhorn.
Cassell's Guide to Paris. Illustrated.
Cassell's Guide to London. With Plans and Woodcuts.
Cassell's Pictorial Guide to the Clyde. With Coloured Plates and Maps.
Pictorial Practical Gardening. By W. P. Wright Illustrated. *Cloth, 1s. 6d.*
Dainty Breakfasts, The Dictionary of. By Phyllis Browne.
Incubators and Chicken Rearing Appliances. How to Make and Use Them. Illustrated.
The Passing of the Dragon. By F. Jay Creagh.
Clear Waters. By Rev. F. Langbridge, M.A. Illustrated. Net.
John Drummond Fraser. By "Philalethes." A Study of Jesuit Intrigue in the Church of England. *Cheap Edition.*
Life Assurance Explained. By Wilson Schooling, F.R.S. *Cloth, 1s. 6d.*
Miniature Cyclopedia, Cassell's. Containing 30,000 Subjects. Cloth. *Cheap Edition, limp cloth. Also cloth gilt, 1s. 6d.*
Practical Pictorial Fruit Growing. By W. P. Wright. Illustrated. *Also cloth, 1s. 6d.*
Cookery for Common Ailments. *Cheap Edition, limp cloth.*
Vegetarian Cookery. By A. G. Payne. *Cheap Edition.*
Cookery, Cassell's Shilling.
Choice Dishes at Small Cost. By A. G. Payne.
A Year's Cookery. By Phyllis Browne. *Cheap Edition, limp cloth.* (Also illustrated cloth edition, 2s.)
Notable Shipwrecks. *Cheap Edition.* Revised and Enlarged. Limp cloth. (Also illustrated edition, 3s. 6d.)
Cassell's Approved Metric Sheets. Two Coloured Sheets, 40in. by 30in., illustrating 13 Designs and Explanations the Metric System. Each. (Also mounted with rollers, 3s. each; or the two on one sheet with rollers, 5s.)
The Governor's Guide to Windsor Castle. By the Most Noble the Marquis of Lorne, K.T. Profusely Illustrated. *Cloth. Also on cloth boards, gilt edges, 2s.*
Popular Control of the Liquor Traffic. By Dr. E. R. L. Gould. With an Introduction by the Rt. Hon. J. Chamberlain. M.P.
Cassell's Guide to Employment in the Civil Service. Revised Edition. *Paper. Also on cloth, 1s. 6d.*
Beneath the Banner; Being Narratives of Noble Lives and Brave Deeds. By F. J. Cross. Illus. *New and Enlarged Edition.* Cloth limp. (Also cloth gilt, gilt edges, 2s.)
Good Morning! Good Night! Morning and Evening Readings for Children. By F. J. Cross. Illustrated. Limp cloth. (Also cloth boards, 2s.)
The Letters of "Vetus" on the Administration of the War Office.
In a Coming Tower. By H. O. Arnold-Forster, M.A. (*See also 6d.*)
An Address in School Hygiene. By Clement Dukes, M.D.
Bits and Bearing-Reins, and Horses and Harness. By E. F. Flower.
The Old Fairy Tales. With Illustrations. Cloth.
Lawful Wedlock; or, How Shall I Make Sure of a Legal Marriage? By Two Barristers.
Our Sick and How to Take Care of Them; or, Plain Teaching as to Nursing at Home. By a Trained Hospital Nurse. *On cloth, 1s. 6d.*
Our Home Army. By H. O. Arnold-Forster, M.A.
The Dwellings of the Poor. Report of the Mansion House Council, 1896. Illustrated.
The Sugar Convention. By the Rt. Hon. Lord Farrer.
Practical Kennel Guide. By Dr. Gordon Stables.
Etiquette of Good Society. *New Edition.* Edited and Revised by Lady Colin Campbell. (*Also on cloth, 1s. 6d.*)
Photography for Amateurs. By T. C. Hepworth. Illustrated. (*Also on cloth, 1s. 6d.*)
The Victoria Painting Book for Little Folks. With about 300 Illustrations. Suited to for Colouring.
The New "LITTLE FOLKS" Painting Book. Containing nearly 350 Outline Illustrations suitable for Colouring.

ILLUSTRATED OFFICIAL RAILWAY GUIDES.

In Paper. (*Also on cloth, 1s. 6d.*)
London and North Western (*New Edition*).—Great Western.—Midland (*New Edition*).—Great Northern.—Great Eastern (*New Edition*).—London and South Western (*New Edition*).—London, Brighton and South Coast (*New Edition*).—South Eastern and Chatham Railway (*New Edition*). (*1s. also 3d.*)

RELIGIOUS.

"HEART CHORDS." Bound in cloth, red edges. Each.

My Work for God.	My Aids to the Divine Life.
My Emotional Life.	My Sources of Strength.
My Growth in Divine Life.	My Father.
My Hereafter.	My Bible.
My Walk with God.	My Comfort in Sorrow.

HELPS TO BELIEF. Edited by Canon Teignmouth-Shore, M.A.
Miracles. By the Rev. Brownlow Maitland, M.A.
The Atonement. By William Connor Magee, D.D., late Archbishop of York.
Sermons Preached in Memory of the Rt. Hon. W. E. Gladstone in Hawarden Parish, May 22, 1898.
Shortened Church Services and Hymns.

1/4

British Museum, The Bible Student in the. By the Rev. C. J. Ellicott, M.A. *New and Revised Edition.*
Tiny Tots. A Magazine for the Very Little Ones. Set in Bold Type and Profusely Illustrated. Annual Volume. (*Also 1s. 6d.*)

1/6

National Library Edition of Shakespeare's Plays. 37 Vols. Bound in leather. Net each.
The Sick and Wounded in South Africa. By Mr. Frederick Charles, M.P.
Cassell's "Wild Flowers" Sheets. Each Sheet is mounted on board with cord suspender, and contains ten coloured plates, beautifully reproduced in colours of familiar wild flowers. 12 sheets. Each.

1/6 cont'd.

The Master of Ballantrae. By R. L. Stevenson. With Introduction, Notes, and Glossary by Thos. Cartwright, B.A.
Topsy Turvy Tales. By S. H. Hamer. With 4 Coloured Plates and other Illustrations by Harry B. Neilson.
The Troubadour. Selections from English Verse. Edited and Annotated by Philip Gibbs.
Peter Piper's Peepshow. By S. H. Hamer. With 4 Coloured Plates and other Illustrations by H. B. Neilson and Lewis Baumer.
The Jungle School. By S. H. Hamer. With 4 Coloured Plates and other Illustrations by H. B. Neilson.
Animal Land for Little People. By S. H. Hamer. Illustrated. Coloured boards.
Master Charlie. By C. S. Harrison and S. H. Hamer. Illustrated. Coloured boards.
Micky Magee's Menagerie; or, Strange Animals and their Doings. By S. H. Hamer. With 8 Coloured Plates and other Illustrations by Harry Neilson.
The Ten Travellers. By S. H. Hamer. With Four Coloured Plates and numerous Illustrations by Harry B. Neilson.
Birds, Beasts, and Fishes. By S. H. Hamer. With Four Coloured Plates and numerous Illustrations.
The Little Huguenot. By Max Pemberton. *New Edition.*
Won at the Last Hole. A Golfing Romance. By M. A. Stobart. Illustrated.
French, Cassell's Lessons in. *New and Revised Edition.* In Two Parts. Each. (*Also in One Vol., 2s.*)
Cassell's Lessons in French, Key to.
Lessons in Our Lives; or, Talks at Broadacre Farm. By H. F. Lester, B.A. Illustrated. In Two Parts. Each.
Object Lessons from Nature, for the Use of Schools. By Prof. L. C. Miall. Illustrated. New and enlarged Edition. Two Vols. 1s. each.
Cassell's Poetry for Recitation. Illustrated. 12 Books in One Vol., cloth. (*See also 6d.*)
Guide to Employment for Boys on leaving School. By W. S. Beard, F.R.G.S.
Carpentry Workshop Practice, Forty Lessons in.
Engineering Workshop Practice, Forty Lessons in.
Elementary Chemistry for Science Schools and Classes.
Twilight of Life, The, Words of Counsel and Comfort for the Aged. By John Ellerton, M.A.
Laws of Every-Day Life. By H. O. Arnold-Forster, M.A.
Citizen Reader. By H. O. Arnold-Forster, M.A. Cloth. (*Also a Scottish Edition, cloth, 1s. 6d.*)
Round the Empire. By G. R. Parkin. With a Preface by the Earl of Rosebery, K.G. Fully Illustrated.
Higher Class Readers, Cassell's. Illustrated. Cloth. Each.
The Making of the Home. By Mrs. S. A. Barnett.
Temperance Reader, The. By J. Dennis Hird.
Little Folks' History of England. By Isa Craig-Knox. With 30 Illustrations. Cloth.
French, Key to Cassell's Lessons in. Cloth.
Experimental Geometry, First Elements of. By Paul Bert. Illustrated.
Principles of Perspective as Applied to Model Drawing and Sketching from Nature, The. By George Trowbridge. Cloth, 2s. 6d.
Nursing for the Home and for the Hospital, A Handbook of. By C. J. Wood. (*Also in cloth, 2s.*)
Cassell's Popular Atlas. Containing 24 Coloured Maps.
The World's Lumber Room. By Selina Gaye.
Wonderful Balloon Ascents.
Wonders of Bodily Strength and Skill.

BIBLE BIOGRAPHIES. Illustrated.

The Story of Joseph. By the Rev. George Bainton.
The Story of Moses and Joshua. By the Rev. J. Telford.
The Story of Judges. By the Rev. J. Wycliffe Gedge.
The Story of Samuel and Saul. By the Rev. D. C. Tovey.
The Story of David. By the Rev. J. Wild.
The Story of Jesus. In Verse. By J. R. Macduff, D.D.

THE WORLD IN PICTURES.

Handsomely Illustrated, and elegantly bound.

All the Russias.	Peeps into China.
Glimpses of South America.	The Land of Temples.
Chats about Germany.	The Isles of the Pacific.
	The Eastern Wonderland.

BOOKS BY EDWARD S. ELLIS. Illustrated.

Bear Cavern.	The Daughter of the Chieftain.
Astray in the Forest.	
Captured by Indians.	The Boy Hunters of Kentucky.
Wolf Ear the Indian.	
Red Feather.	

EIGHTEENPENNY STORY BOOKS.

All Illustrated throughout, and bound in cloth gilt.

Bear and Forbear.	Her Wilful Way.
Honour is my Guide.	To School and Away.
Aim at a Sure End.	All in a Castle Fair.
On Board the "Esmeralda."	The Braes of the Brave.
Clare Linton's Friend.	Dolly's Golden Slippers.

1/8

Founders of the Empire. A Biographical Reader Book for School and Home. By Philip Gibbs. Illustrated. (*See also 2s. 6d.*)
In Danger's Hour; or, Stout Hearts and Stirring Deeds. A Book of Adventure for School and Home. With Colquhoun Plates and other Illustrations. (*1s. 6d. also 2d.*)
Cassell's Classical Readers. Vol. I. (*Also Vol. II., 2s. 6d.*)

1/9

Our Great City; or, London the Heart of the Empire. By H. O. Arnold-Forster, M.A. Profusely Illustrated. (*2s. also 2d.*)
Physiology for Schools. By Alfred T. Schofield, M.D., M.R.C.S., &c. Illustrated. Cloth. (*Also in Three Parts, paper covers, 5d. each; or cloth limp, 6d. each.*)

2/- 2/6 cont'd.

EDUCATIONAL.

French Lessons in French. By F. P. de Champlain.
Hand and Eye Training. By G. Ricks, B.Sc. and J. Vaughan. Illustrated. Vol. II., Designing in Cardboard (Vol. III. Colour Work and Design, 3s.)
Historical Cartoons, Cassell's Coloured. Size 45 in. × 35 in. 5s. Each. (Text also.)
Practical Solid Geometry, A Manual of. By William Gordon Ross, Major R.E.
Alphabet, Cassell's Pictorial, and Object Lesson Sheet for Infant Schools. (Also 42 in. 6d.)
Linear Drawing. By E. A. Davidson.
Orthographic and Isometrical Projection.
Building Construction, The Elements of.
Systematic Drawing and Shading. By Charles Ryan.
Jones's Book-keeping. By Theodore Jones. For Schools, 2s.; for the blanks, 1s. (Also in cloth, 2s.) Ruled Books, 2s.
Reading Sheets, Modern. 38 sheets. Each. (Also on linen, with rollers, 5s. each.)

MISCELLANEOUS.

Special Pocket Editions of Ellicott's Commentaries. On thin paper, each. ST. MATTHEW, ST. MARK, ST. LUKE, ST. JOHN.
The Elements of Modern Dressmaking. By Jeanette E. Davis. *New and Revised Edition.*
Advice to Women on the Care of their Health. By Florence Stacpoole. *New and Enlarged Edition.*
Technical Instruction. Edited by Paul N. Hasluck. Vol I., Practical Staircase Joinery. Vol II., Practical Metal Work. Vol III., Practical Gas Fitting. Vol. IV. Practical Draughtsman's Work. Vol. V., Practical Graining and Marbling. Each.
A Gun-Room Ditty Box. By G. Stewart Bowles, with a Preface by Rear-Admiral Lord Charles Beresford.
The London Health Laws. Prepared by the Mansion House Council on the Dwellings of the Poor.
Gea, The Art of Cooking by. By Marie Jenny Sugg. Illustrated.
Cassell's Popular Cookery. With Coloured Plates.
How Dante Climbed the Mountain. By R.E. Selfe. Illustrated. **With Dante in Paradise.** By R. E. Selfe. Illustrated.
Cassell's Book of In-door Amusements, Card Games, and Fireside Fun. Illustrated.
The North-West Passage by Land. By Lord Milton and Dr. Cheadle. *Cheap Edition.*
"Little Folks" Sunday Book.

TWO-SHILLING STORY BOOKS.

Illustrated. Crown 8vo, handsomely bound in cloth gilt.

Adam Hepburn's Vow. A Tale of Kirk and Covenant.	The Mystery of Master Max
The Lost Vestal.	Uncle Silvio's Secret
Fairway Island	Wrong from the First.
Fluffy and Jack.	Daisy's Dilemma.
	A Self-willed Family.

BOOKS BY EDWARD S. ELLIS. Illustrated.

Blazing Arrow.	In the Days of the Pioneers.
Chieftain and Scout.	Shod with Silence.
Iron Heart: War Chief of the Iroquois.	The Phantom of the River.
	The Great Cattle Trail.
Red Jacket: The Last of the Senecas	The Path in the Ravine.
	The Young Ranchers.
In Red Indian Trails	The Hunters of the Ozark.
Uncrowning a King	The Camp in the Mountains.
Two Boys in Wyoming	The Last War Trail.
Scouts and Comrades, or Tecumseh, Chief of the Shawanons	Ned in the Woods.
	Ned on the River.
	Ned in the Block House. A Story of Pioneer Life in Kentucky.
Klondike Nuggets	The Lost Trail.
Cowmen and Rustlers.	Camp-Fire and Wigwam.
A Strange Craft and its Wonderful Voyage	Footprints in the Forest.
	Down the Mississippi.
Pontiac, Chief of the Ottawas. A Tale of the Siege of Detroit.	Lost in the Wilds.
	The Rubber Hunters.

CASSELL'S MINIATURE POETS.

Two Volumes in one, cloth gilt, gilt edges.
Milton. Sheridan.

"WANTED—A KING" SERIES.

Cheap Edition. Illustrated.

Two Old Ladies, Two Foolish Fairies, and a Tom Cat. By Maggie Browne.
Fairy Tales in Other Lands. By Julia Goddard.
Wanted—a King; or, How Merle set the Nursery Rhymes to Rights. By Maggie Browne.

2/6

THE "CROSS AND CROWN" SERIES.

With Four Illustrations in each Book, printed on a Line.

Through Trial to Triumph. | **By Fire and Sword: A Story**
Strong to Suffer. | **of the Huguenots**
Freedom's Sword. A Story of the Days of Wallace and Bruce.

HALF-CROWN GIFT BOOKS.

POPULAR VOLUMES FOR YOUNG PEOPLE.

Whys and other Whys; or, Curious Creatures and their Tales. By S. H. Hamer. With 104 Sections by Harry B. Neilson. (4s. Cloth, 3s. 6d.)
The Queen's Scarlet. By George Manville Fenn.
An Old Boy's Yarns; or, School Tales for Past and Present Boys. Illustrated by Harold Avery.
Told Out of School; or, Humorous Yarns of School Life and Boyhood. By A. J. Daniels. Illustrated.
To Punish the Czar: A Story of the Crimea. By Horace Hutchinson. Illustrated.
Lost Among White Africans. A Boy's Adventures on the Upper Congo. By David Ker. Illustrated.
The White House at Inch Gow. By Sarah Pitt. Illustrated.
The Master of the Strong Hearts. A Story of Custer's Last Rally. By E. S. Brooks. Illustrated.
Pleasant Work for Busy Fingers; or, Kindergarten at Home. By Maggie Browne. Illustrated.
Little Mother Bunch. By Mrs. Molesworth. Illustrated.
Pictures of School Life and Boyhood. Selected from the best Authors. Edited by Percy Fitzgerald, M.A.
Perils Afloat and Brigands Ashore. By Alfred Elwes.
Heroes of Every-Day Life. By Laura Lane. Illustrated.
Heroes of the Indian Empire. By Ernest Foster.
At the South Pole. By the late W. H. G. Kingston.
To the Death. By R. D. Chetwode.
Cost of a Mistake. By Sarah Pitt.
Rogues of the Fiery Cross. By S. Walkey. Illustrated.
Lost so Du Corrig; or, Twixt Earth and Ocean. By Standish O'Grady. With 8 full page Illustrations.
With the Redskins on the War Path. By S. Walkey.

EDUCATIONAL.

Our Great City; or London the Heart of the Empire. By H. O. Arnold-Forster, M.A.
The Coming of the Kilogram; or, the Battle of the Standards. By H. O. Arnold-Forster, M.A. Illustrated. (Cloth.)
Farm Crops. By Professor Wrightson. Illustrated.
The Young Citizen; or, Lessons in our Laws. By H. F. Lester, B.A. Fully Illustrated. (Also in two parts, 1s. 6d. each.)
Sculpture, A Primer of. By E. R. Mullins.
Numerical Examples in Practical Mechanics and Machine Design. By R. G. Blaine, M.E. *New Edition, Revised and Enlarged.* With 79 Illustrations.
Latin Primer (The New). By Prof. J. P. Postgate.
Latin Prose for Lower Forms. By M. A. Bayfield, M.A.
Chemistry, The Public School. By J. H. Anderson, M.A.
Oil Painting, A Manual of. By the Hon. John Collier. Cloth.
French Grammar, Marlborough. Arrange and Compiled by Rev. J. F. Bright, M.A. (See "Answers," 3s. 6d.)
Algebra, Manual of. By Galbraith and Haughton. Part I. Cloth. (Complete, 7s. 6d.)
Euclid. Books I. II. III. By Galbraith and Haughton. Books IV. V. VI. By Galbraith and Haughton.
Optics. By Galbraith and Haughton. *Entirely New and Enlarged Edition.*
"Model Joint" Wall Sheets, for Instruction in Manual Training. By S. Barter. Eight Sheets. Each.
This World of Ours. By H. O. Arnold-Forster, M.A. Being Introductory Lessons to the Study of Geography. *Cheap Edition.*
Scarlet and Blue; or, Songs for Soldiers and Sailors. By John Farmer. (See also 5s.)

MISCELLANEOUS.

Alfred Shaw, Cricketer; His Career and Reminiscences. By A. W. Pullin. With a Steel Portrait by A. J. Calvin.
The Century Science Series. Edited by Sir Henry E. Roscoe, D.Sc., F.R.S. Each. (List sent on application.)
Encyclopædia of the Game of Whist. By Sir William Laurie Smith, Bart.
Sir Robert Peel. By Lord Rosebery.
Founders of the Empire. By Philip Gibbs. (Also 2s. 6d.)
The New Penny Magazine. With 650 Illustrations. In Quarterly Volumes. Each.
A Book of Absurdities. For Children of from Seven Years of Age to Seventy. By an Old Volunteer.
Liquor Legislation in the United States and Canada. By E. L. Fanshawe, with the latest Temperance Statistics.
Field Naturalist's Handbook, The. By the Rev. J. G. and Theodore Wood. *Cheap Edition.*
The Art of Making and Using Sketches. From the French of G. Fraipont. By Clara Bell. With Fifty Illustrations.
National Railways. An Argument for State Purchase. By James Hole.
Church Reform in Spain and Portugal. By the Rev. H. E. Noyes, D.D. Illustrated.

Cassell & Company's Classified Price List.

Cassell & Company, Limited, Ludgate Hill, London; Paris, New York and Melbourne.

10/6 *cont'd.*

The Automobile: Its Construction and Management. Translated from the French of Gérard Lavergne, Edited and Revised by H. N. Hart. Illustrated. *Net.*

Moses and Geology; or, The Harmony of the Bible with Science. By the Rev. Samuel Kinns, Ph.D., F.R.A.S. With 91 Illustrations. *(See also new cheaper and popular Edition.)*

Europe, A History of Modern. By C. A. Fyffe, M.A., late Fellow of University College, Oxford. *Cheap Edition.* In One Vol. *(Also Library Edition.* Illustrated, 3 Vols., 7s. 6d. each.)

The Doré Don Quixote. With about 400 Illustrations by Gustave Doré. *Cheap Edition.*

Fulton's Book of Pigeons. With Standards for Judging. Edited by Lewis Wright. Revised, Enlarged, and Supplemented by the Rev. W. F. Lumley. With Fifty Full-page Illustrations. *Popular Edition.* In One Vol. *(Also Original Edition, with 50 Coloured Plates and Numerous Engravings, 21s.)*

Electric Current, The. By Professor Walmsley. Illustrated.

Picturesque Europe. (The British Islands.) Contains 13 exquisite Steel Plates, and about 200 Original Engravings, by the best Artists. Two Vols. in One. *(See also 21s.)*

Elements of Machine Construction and Drawing. By Prof. Henry J. Spooner, C.E., etc., and Edward de Lorey, A.M.I.M.E. Two Vols. Size 11½ x 9½ inches. In One Vol. Cloth. *(See also 21s.)*

R. M. S. Curves (Scaled Curve Templates). By Prof. R. H. Smith. 95 in box with explanatory pamphlet.

Dictionary of Phrase and Fable. By the Rev. Dr. Brewer. *Authoric Parts and Larger Authorised Edition.* (Also 3s. 6d. and 10s. 6d. morocco.) Two Vols., 10s.

Building Construction Plates. A series of 40 drawings. Cloth. 100 Copies of any plate may be obtained in quantities of not less than one dozen, price 2s. 6d. per dozen.)

"Six Hundred Years"; or, Historical Sketches of Eminent Men and Women who have more or less come into contact with the Abbey and Church of Holy Trinity, Minories, from 1293 to 1893, including some account of the Incumbents, the Parish, the Plate, &c. With 65 Illustrations. By the Rev. Dr. Samuel Kinns, F.R.A.S., &c. &c. *Net.*

Encyclopædic Dictionary, The. A New and Original Work of Reference to the Words in the English Language. Complete in Fourteen Divisional Vols. Each.

Poultry, The Book of. By Lewis Wright. *Popular Edition.* With Illustrations on Wood. *(See also 9s.)*

Gun and its Development, The. With Notes on Shooting. By W. W. Greener. *Ninth and Entirely New Edition.*

Sun, The Story of the. By Sir Robert Ball, LL.D. With Eight Coloured Plates and other Illustrations. *Cheap Edition.*

Heavens, The Story of the. By Sir Robert Ball, LL.D. *Popular Edition.* Illustrated by Chromo Plates and Wood Engravings.

12/-

Britain at Work. A Pictorial Description of our National Industries. Written by popular authors and containing nearly 700 Illustrations.

Cathedrals, Abbeys, and Churches of England and Wales. Descriptive, Historical, Pictorial. *Popular Edition.* With nearly 500 Original Illustrations. Two Vols. The Set.

Her Majesty's Tower. By Hepworth Dixon. 2 Vols. With Coloured Plates.

Our Railways. Their Origin, Development, Incident, and Romance. By John Pendleton. Two Vols. Illustrated.

Social England. Edited by H. D. Traill. Six Vols. of *New Illustrated Edition. Net.*

Living London: its Work and its Play, its Humour and its Pathos, its Sights and its Scenes. Edited by George R. Sims. Vols. I. and II. Profusely Illustrated.

The Nation's Pictures. Vols. I. and II. Each consisting of beautiful Coloured Reproductions of some of the finest Modern Paintings in the Picture Galleries of Great Britain. With Descriptive Text.

12/6

Aconcagua and Tierra del Fuego. A Record of Climbing, Travel, and Exploration. By Sir Martin Conway. With numerous Illustrations from Photographs. *Net.*

British Nigeria. By Lieut.-Col. Mockler-Ferryman. With 16 Illustrations. *Net.*

"The Shop," The Story of the Royal Military Academy. By Capt. Goggisberg, R.E. With numerous Illustrations and Eight Coloured Plates. *New and Revised Edition. Net.*

Milton's Paradise Lost. Illustrated by Doré. *Cheap Edition.* In One Vol. 10s. 6d. *(See also 7s. 6d. and 21s.)*

Newman Hall. An Autobiography. With Portrait and Illustrations.

14/-

Social England. Edited by H. D. Traill, D.C.L., and J. S. Mann, M.A. Vols. II. and III. of *New Illustrated Edition. Net.*

15/-

The Land of the Dons. By Leonard Williams. With about 40 Illustrations. *Net.*

The Life of Lives: Further Studies in the Life of Christ. By Dean Farrar.

"Graven in the Rock"; or, the Historical Accuracy of the Bible. By the Rev. Dr. Samuel Kinns, F.R.A.S., &c. &c. With Numerous Illustrations. *Library Edition.* Two Vols.

The Doré Bible. With 200 Full-page Illustrations by Gustave Doré. *(Also in leather binding, price on application.)*

15/- *cont'd.*

The Nation's Pictures. Vols. I. and II., each containing 48 beautiful Coloured Reproductions of some of the finest Modern Paintings in the Picture Galleries of Great Britain. With Descriptive Text. Half Leather. *(See also 12s.)*

Shakspere, The Royal. Three Vols. The Set.

16/-

Living London. Half Leather. *(See also 12s.)*

The History of "Punch." By M. H. Spielmann. With nearly 170 Illustrations, Portraits, and Facsimiles. In One Vol. Also *Large Paper Edition*, £2 2s.

Rivers of Great Britain. Descriptive, Historical, Pictorial.

The Royal River: The Thames from Source to Sea. With Several Hundred Original Illustrations. *Popular Edition.*

Rivers of the East Coast. With numerous highly finished Engravings. *Popular Edition. (See also 42s.)*

Rivers of the South and West Coasts.

18/-

Early Christianity and Paganism. By Very Rev. H. D. M. Spence, D.D. Illustrated. *Net.*

Picturesque America. With Steel Plates and Wood Engravings. *Popular Edition.* Complete in Four Vols. Each. *(See also £6 12s.)*

20/-

London, Greater. *Library Edition.* Two Vols. *(See also 4s. 6d.)*

21/-

Sights and Scenes in Oxford City and University. Illustrated with upwards of 100 Plates after original Photographs. In one Vol.

Mysteries of Police and Crime. A General Survey of Wrongdoing and its Pursuit. By Major Arthur Griffiths, one of H.M. Inspectors of Prisons. Two Vols. The Set.

With Nature and a Camera. By Richard Kearton, F.Z.S. With a Special introduction and 180 Pictures from Photographs direct from Nature by C. Kearton. *(See also 7s. 6d.)*

British Birds' Nests: How, Where, and When to Find and Identify Them. By Richard Kearton, F.Z.S. With nearly 130 Illustrations of Nests, Eggs, Young, etc., from Photographs direct from Nature by C. Kearton. *(See also 7s. 6d.)*

Memoirs and Correspondence of Lyon Playfair, First Lord Playfair of St. Andrews. By Sir Wemyss Reid. With Two Portraits. *(See also 7s. 6d.)*

Dante's Inferno, Purgatory, and Paradise, and Milton's Paradise Lost. Three Vols. Illustrated by Doré. In Case.

Magazine of Art, The. Yearly Volume. With Exquisite Photogravures, and about 500 Illustrations from Original Drawings, and a series of full-page Plates.

Annals of Westminster Abbey. By E. T. Bradley (Mrs. A. Murray Smith). Illustrated by W. Hatherell, R.I., H. M. Paget, and Francis S. Walker, R.H.A., A.R.I.E. Royal 4to. With a Preface by the Dean of Westminster and a Chapter on the Abbey Buildings by J. T. Micklethwaite, F.S.A. *Cheap Edition.*

Familiar Garden Flowers. *Popular Edition.* In Five Vols. With 40 Full-page Coloured Plates in each Vol. In paste grain, Five Vols. in box or match. *Net. (See also 9s. 6d.)*

Poultry, The Illustrated Book of. By Lewis Wright. *New and Revised Edition in preparation.* With Fifty Coloured Plates, gilt edges. *(See also 9s.)*

Health, The Book of. Cloth. *(Also in roxburgh, 25s.)*

Milton's Paradise Lost. Illustrated with Full-page Drawings by Gustave Doré. *(See also 7s. 6d. and 10s. 6d.)*

Shakespeare, The Plays of. Edited by Prof. Henry Morley. Thirteen Vols., in box, cloth; or 39 Vols., cloth, in box. *(Also half-morocco, with Index, 42s.)*

RELIGIOUS WORKS.

Cassell's Guinea Bible. With 900 Illustrations and Coloured Maps. Royal 4to, and our French Antique with Corners and Clasps, 25s. 6d.

Farrar's Life of Christ, Life and Work of St. Paul, and Early Days of Christianity, in uniform binding. Cloth, gilt top, in cloth box. The set. *(See also 3s. 6d. and 6s.)*

Farrar's Life and Work of St. Paul. ILLUSTRATED EDITION. *(See also 7s. 6d., 12s. 6d., 15s., 24s., and 42s.)*

Early Days of Christianity, The. By the Very Rev. Dean Farrar, D.D., F.R.S. *Library Edition.* Two Vols., demy 8vo. *(See also 3s. 6d., 7s. 6d., 12s., 21s., and 42s.)*

24/-

Farrar's Life and Work of St. Paul. *Library Edition.* Two Vols., cloth. *(See also 3s. 6d., 7s. 6d., 12s., 21s., and 42s.)*

25/-

Familiar Wild Flowers. *Popular Edition.* In Six Vols. With 40 Full-page Coloured Plates in each Vol. In paste grain, Six Vols. in box or match. *Net. (See also 9s. 6d.)*

Horses and Dogs. By O. Eerelman. With Descriptive Text. Translated from the Dutch by Clara Bell. With Photogravure Frontispiece, 12 Coloured Collotypes, and several full-page and other Engravings in the Text. *Net.*

British Empire Map of the World. By G. R. Parkin and J. G. Bartholomew, F.R.G.S. Mounted on Cloth, with Rollers or folded.

MAGAZINES AND SERIAL PUBLICATIONS.

M., Monthly.   **W.,** Weekly.   **F.,** Fortnightly.

MAGAZINES.

Cassell's Magazine. Monthly, 6d.
The Quiver. Monthly, 6d.
Little Folks. Monthly, 6d.
The Magazine of Art. New Series. Monthly, 1s.
Chums. Monthly, 6d. (Also W., 1d.)

Cassell's Saturday Journal. Monthly, 6d. (Also W., 1d.)
The New Penny Magazine. Monthly, 6d. (Also W., 1d.)
Tiny Tots. Monthly, 1d.

WEEKLY JOURNALS.

Work. The Illustrated Journal for Mechanics. W., 1d.; M., 6d.
Building World. The Illustrated Journal for the Building Trades. W., 1d.; M., 6d.

The Gardener. A Weekly Journal for all who cultivate Flowers, Fruit, and Vegetables. W., 1d.; M., 6d.

SERIAL PUBLICATIONS.

Annals of Surgery. M., 2s.
Boer War. F., 6d. net.
Book of the Cat. M., 1s. net.
Biblewomen and Nurses. M., 2d.
Britain at Work. F., 7d. net.
Butterflies and Moths. F., 7d. net.
Dictionary of Practical Gardening. M., 7d. net.
Electricity in the Service of Man. M., 6d.
Encyclopædic Dictionary. W., 6d. net.
Handy Man's Book. M. 6d.

Live Stock. M., 1s. net.
Living London. F., 7d. net.
Nation's Pictures, The. F., 7d. net.
Practitioner, The. M., 2s.
Social England. F., 1s. net.
Sports of the World. F., 7d. net.
Sporting Pictures. M., 1s. net.
Story of Our Planet. M., 6d.
Wild Flowers, Familiar. F., 6d. net.

Letts's Diaries and other Time-Saving Publications are published exclusively by CASSELL & COMPANY, and particulars will be forwarded post free on application to the Publishers.

CASSELL & COMPANY, Limited, *Ludgate Hill, London; Paris, New York and Melbourne.*